Jack
and the
Beanstalk

Key sound long oo spellings: ew, oo, u
Secondary sounds: ie, ow, ea

Written by Nick Page
Illustrated by Clare Fennell

Reading with phonics

How to use this book

The **Reading with phonics** series helps you to have fun with your child and to support their learning of phonics and reading. It is aimed at children who have learned the letter sounds and are building confidence in their reading.

Each title in the series focuses on a different key sound. The entertaining retelling of the story repeats this sound frequently, and the different spellings for the sound are highlighted in red type. The first activity at the back of the book provides practice in reading and using words that contain this sound. The key sound for **Jack and the Beanstalk** is the **long oo.**

Start by reading the story to your child, asking them to join in with the refrain in bold. Next, encourage them to read the story with you. Give them a hand to decode tricky words.

Now look at the activity pages at the back of the book. These are intended for you and your child to enjoy together. Most are not activities to complete in pencil or pen, but by reading and talking or pointing.

The **Key sound** pages focus on one sound, and on the various different groups of letters that produce that sound. Encourage your child to read the different letter groups and complete the activity, so they become more aware of the variety of spellings there are for the same sound.

The **Letters together** pages look at three pairs or groups of letters and at the sounds they make as they work together. Help your child to read the words and trace the route on the word maps.

Rhyme is used a lot in these retellings. Whatever stage your child has reached in their learning of phonics, it is always good practice for them to listen carefully for sounds and find words that rhyme. The pages on **Rhyming words** take six words from the story and ask children to read and find other words that rhyme with them.

The **Sight words** pages focus on a number of sight words that occur regularly but can nonetheless be challenging. Many of these words are not sounded out following the rules of phonics and the easiest thing is for children to learn them by sight, so that they do not worry about decoding them. These pages encourage children to retell the story, practicing sight words as they do so.

The **Picture dictionary** page asks children to focus closely on nine words from the story. Encourage children to look carefully at each word, cover it with their hand, write it on a separate piece of paper, and finally, check it!

Do not complete all the activities at once – doing one each time you read will ensure that your child continues to enjoy the stories and the time you are spending together. **Have fun!**

Jack Pott and his mom
had a poor life, not much fun.
Food was scarce for those two
and their cow, called Little Moo.

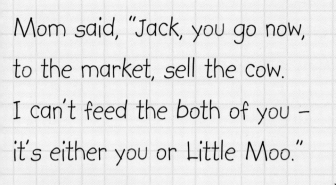

Mom said, "Jack, you go now,
to the market, sell the cow.
I can't feed the both of you –
it's either you or Little Moo."

Fee-fi-foo-fum!
Jack Pott, what have you done?

A lady said, "Don't be blue.
I will buy that cow from you.
Can't pay cash – beyond my means –
instead, do use my magic beans."

Moo!

Back home, young Jack Pott
showed his mom the beans he got.
"You've been fooled!" his mother said.
"Throw them out and go to bed!"

Fee-fi-foo-fum!
Jack Pott, what have you done?

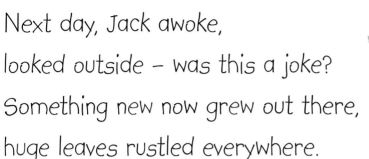

Next day, Jack awoke,
looked outside – was this a joke?
Something new now grew out there,
huge leaves rustled everywhere.

"Magic beans!" said Jack. "It's true!"
And now a beanstalk filled the view,
soared into the clouds so high,
climbing through the bright blue sky.

Fee-fi-foo-fum!
Jack Pott, what have you done?

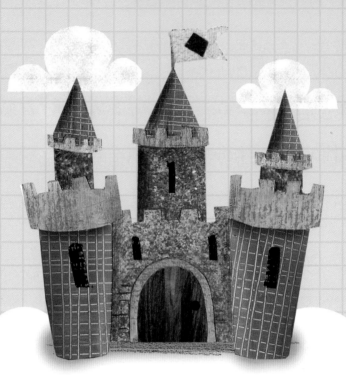

Jack climbed up, and at the top,
a sight to make his eyes go "pop"!
A castle with huge rooms inside,
where everything was giant-sized.

Jack looked, and – behold! –
a blue goose laying eggs of gold.
"Rescue me!" honks the goose.
Jack says, "How could I refuse?"

Fee-fi-foo-fum!
Jack Pott, what have you done?

Boom!

Then – BOOM! – through the door,
a giant looms, begins to roar:
"Fee-fi-FOO-fum,
I smell the blood of an Englishman.
Be he alive, or be he dead,
I'll use his bones to grind my bread."
Jack says, "What a brute!"
And past the giant's boots he scoots.

Fee-fi-foo-fum!
Jack Pott, what have you done?

Jack runs off with his loot
and the giant in pursuit,
to the beanstalk with the goose,
while the giant screams abuse:

"Fee-fi-FOO-fum!
Run, you puny human, run!
Do you know what I will do?
I'll use you in a human stew!"

Fee-fi-foo-fum!
Jack Pott, what have you done?

15

16

Back home, Jack's mom says,
"You were grounded! Back to bed!"
"Quick!" says Jack. "No time to lose!
Cut the beanstalk! Hold this goose!"

Jack tells her all the facts.
"Ooh!" she says. "Use this axe."
From above, a voice booms clear:
"I can see your house from here!"

Fee-fi-foo-fum!
Jack Pott, what have you done?

Ooh!

Jack Pott starts to chop,

then a voice comes from up top:

"Fee-fi-FOO-fum,

I smell the blood of an English mom!

In a goulash or fondue,

I'll have her boiled or barbecued!"

CHOP! CHOP! Cracks appear!

Goose shouts, "TIMBER! All stand clear!"

Fee-fi-foo-fum!

Jack Pott, what have you done?

Timber!

19

CREAK! CRACK! Suddenly,
the beanstalk falls like a toppled tree.
With a swooshing-whooshing sound,
the giant crashes to the ground.

BUMP! THUMP! Completely dead.

"He's been grounded," Jack's mom said.

Jack laughs, "What a hoot!"

Then he shows his mom the loot!

Fee-fi-foo-fum!

Jack Pott, what have you done?

21

"Ooh, Jack," said his mom.

"What a super-duper son!"

Jack knew what to do,

so he bought back Little Moo,

built a house for them all,

made the goose a swimming pool.

But Jack sometimes dreams . . .

"Maybe I should plant more beans?"

Fee-fi-foo-fum!
Jack Pott, what have you done?

Key sound

There are several different groups of letters that make the **long oo** sound. Practice them by following the different **long oo** coins to help Jack find the treasure.

true

brute

grew

chew

pool

fool

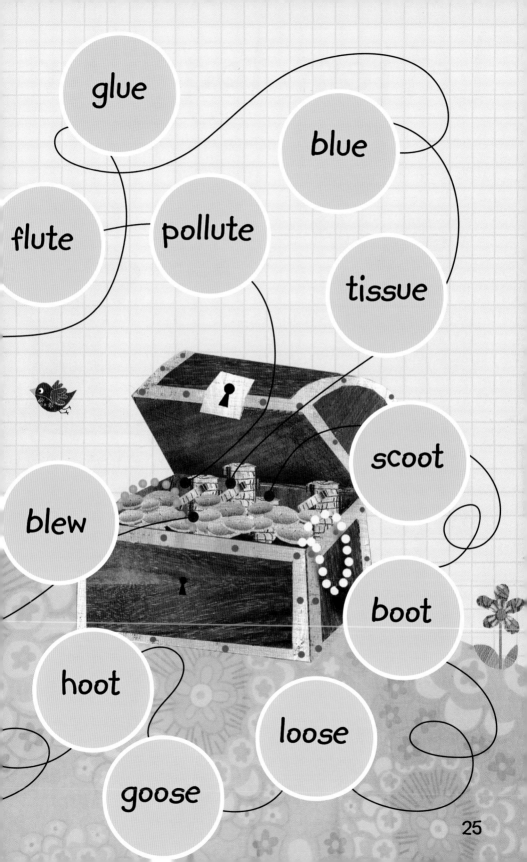

glue

blue

flute

pollute

tissue

scoot

blew

boot

hoot

loose

goose

25

Letters together

Look at these pairs of letters and say the sounds they make.

ie **ow** **ea**

Follow the words that contain **ie** to help the giant find the thief!

ie

chief

waves

grief

brief

lost

from

shriek

jumps

right

thief

Follow the words that contain **ow** to help Mom find Jack's cow.

the

ow

other

owl

shower

clown

flower

frown

lots

cow .... down

Follow the words that contain **ea** to help Jack find the beanstalk.

ea

bean

leaf

suddenly

sea

please

other

beanstalk

gold

Rhyming words

Read the words in the flowers and point to other words that rhyme with them.

now	cow	leaves
how		blue

mean	bean	lean
gold		egg

pool	brute	bread
flute		chute

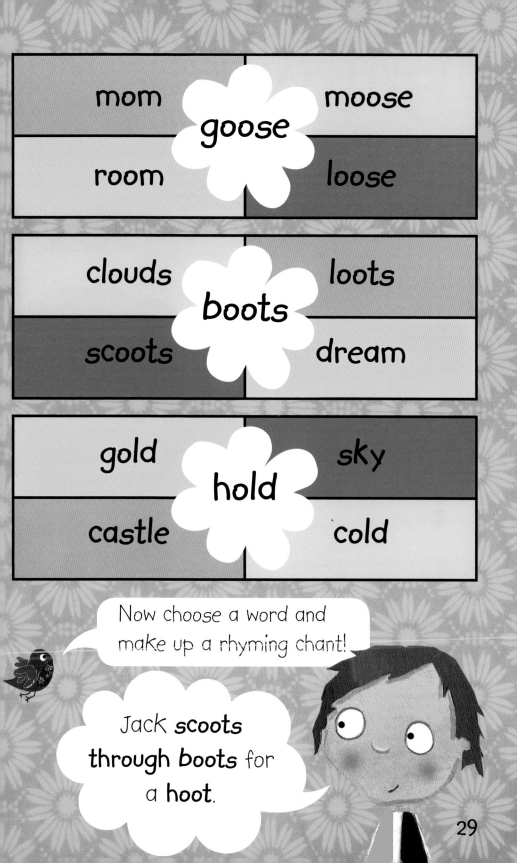

Sight words

Many common words can be difficult to sound out. Practice them by reading these sentences about the story. Now make more sentences using other sight words.

Jack sold his cow **for** magic beans.

Jack climbed **down** the beanstalk.

Jack found a castle **in** the sky.

A beanstalk grew in the **garden**.

mom • when • in

• cried • keep • room • giant • down • even • from • for

Jack's **mom** threw the beans out the window.

Jack **found** a blue goose.

The **giant** chased Jack.

They cut down the beanstalk!

Suddenly, the giant fell down.

say • found • couldn't • head • town • around • every • garden • fast • only • many

laughed • they • much • suddenly • told • great • why •

Picture dictionary

Look carefully at the pictures and the words.
Now cover the words, one at a time.
Can you remember how to write them?

axe   beans   beanstalk

castle   clouds   giant

gold   goose   loot